Part-time Princess

Deborah Underwood

illustrated by Cambria Evans

Disney • Hyperion Books
New York

Text copyright © 2013 by Deborah Underwood • Illustrations copyright © 2013 by Cambria Evans

All rights reserved. Published by Disney • Hyperion Books, an imprint of Disney Book Group. No part of this book may be reproduced or transmitted in any form or by any means, electronic or mechanical, including photocopying, recording, or by any information storage and retrieval system, without written permission from the publisher. For information address Disney • Hyperion Books, 114 Fifth Avenue, New York, New York 10011-5690.

Printed in Singapore • First Edition • 1 3 5 7 9 10 8 6 4 2 • F850-6835-5-13015

This book is set in Yana • The art was created with a mix of mediums and colored digitally • Book design by Whitney Manger

Library of Congress Cataloging-in-Publication Data

Underwood, Deborah.
 Part-time princess / written by Deborah Underwood ; illustrated by Cambria Evans.—1st ed.
   p. cm.
 Summary: A girl escapes her annoying little brother and the drudgery of school and home life
when she travels to a magical kingdom each night and embarks on a series of adventures.
 ISBN 978-1-4231-2485-6
 [1. Family life—Fiction. 2. Bedtime—Fiction. 3. Princesses—Fiction.] I. Evans, Cambria, ill. II. Title.
 PZ7.U4193Par 2012
 [E]—dc23   2011014641

Reinforced binding • Visit www.disneyhyperionbooks.com

For Sophie and Sarah, with love—D.U.

To my favorite twin, Jen Merrill,
and to Princesses Elsa and Lola—C.E.

During the day, I am a regular girl.

I have to take spelling tests.

My little brother
breaks my crayons.

I'm not allowed
to jump off the high dive

or stomp in puddles.

But at night, after Mom
kisses me and tucks me in . . .

I become a princess.

At the stroke of midnight,
a sparkling crown appears on my head.

A magical staircase rolls down from my window.

My coach awaits!

I tell the driver to hurry, because . . .

. . . there is usually an emergency.

When we arrive,
I get right to work.

A real princess
can slide down a fire pole
in a frilly skirt.

No one *dreams* of telling her
it's too dangerous.

Princess to the rescue!
I save the kingdom, as usual.

When I lasso the dragon, the townspeople cheer.
"Lock him up!" they yell.

But I have a different idea.

I invite the dragon to tea.

It turns out he's just crabby because his little brother melted his crayons.

today's
TEA

PEPPERMINT

Menu
special : FRESH-PICKED STRAWBERRIES
BERRY CUPCAKES · GOOSEBERRY PIE
LEMON TARTS · PINK CAKE · MACARONS
TRIPLE CHOCOLATE CHIP COOKIES · CRUMPETS
DONUTS WITH SPRINKLES · PETITE SANDWICHES

All he needs is a little cheering up
(and a fresh box of crayons).

Then I go to school.

A princess studies
magical beasts,

fencing,

and circus arts.

I pass my trapeze test with flying colors.

Next, it's time for lunch.

A queen from a faraway land is my guest.
We eat three slices of pink cake.
Each.

The frogs in the Royal Mud Puddle
invite us for a game of leapfrog.

Of course we say yes.

Then it's time to get cleaned up
because the Royal Ball is tonight!

I dive into in a giant tub with hot and cold running bubbles. And a dolphin.

The queen and I choose the perfect clothes.
Her dress looks like the sky at sunset.

My gown shimmers like starlight.

Everyone gathers for the ball.
Even a troop of big, hairy trolls.

Some of my subjects are frightened.

Not me, because I know
that trolls love to dance.

"Strike up the band!" I call.

The ball is saved!

I dance with the head troll . . .

and a *very* handsome prince.

Maybe I'll marry him when I grow up.
But right now I'm too busy.

I have lots of fires to fight.
(And lots of dragons to cheer up.)

After a long night,
I head home and
curl up in my own bed.

In the morning, I find sparkles in my hair.
"You look tired," Mom says.
"Did you have a busy night?"

She winks.

There are sparkles in her hair too!

That night, she tucks me in.
"I'll see you later," I whisper.

And I do.